WHEN A MAN LOVES YOU

ALAN ANNES

WHEN A MAN LOVES YOU

What He Keeps Inside

ReadersMagnet, LLC

When a Man Loves You: What He Keeps Inside
Copyright © 2021 by Alan Annes

Published in the United States of America
ISBN Paperback: 978-1-954371-55-2
ISBN Hardback: 978-1-954371-56-9
ISBN eBook: 978-1-954371-54-5

All rights reserved. No part of this publication may be reproduced, stored in a retrieval system or transmitted in any way by any means, electronic, mechanical, photocopy, recording or otherwise without the prior permission of the author except as provided by USA copyright law.

ReadersMagnet, LLC
10620 Treena Street, Suite 230 | San Diego, California, 92131 USA
1.619. 354. 2643 | www.readersmagnet.com

Book design copyright © 2021 by ReadersMagnet, LLC. All rights reserved.
Cover design by Kent Gabutin
Interior design by Renalie Malinao

INTRODUCTION

Here is my second book of short poems to share my thoughts and imagination about love and romance. Growing up I read a lot of books about everything I could find to read Science, Philosophy, Politics, History, Music, Romance Novels and Comic Books. I enjoy watching Action Flicks, Comedies, Love Stories, Science Fiction and Romantic Comedies. Sometimes I would try to imagine how the characters in books and movies felt then write a short poem. Some of the poems were written from my personal feelings about love and relationships over the years. Read them all and if you like them I have more to share.

Enjoy the poems,
Alan Annes

BABY GIRL

Hey baby girl I just want you so bad.
Sometimes I feel like I am going mad.
I wonder If you will ever be with me.
I need you to help set my heart free.
Each moment as I wait for your text.
Seems like hours until I get the next.
I will lay my heart right out on the line.
If that is what it takes to make you mine.
I do not know if you feel the way I do.
I am not lying when I say I need you.
Because I will do anything to please you.
Do not know what to say or what to do.
I will just wait till you walk in my door.
I will give you what you want and more.
Seems days passed since the last text.
What should I do baby girl what is next?

LOST NIGHTS

Lost nights I spent awake dreaming about you.
Wishing you would make my dreams come true.
I was up all night just lying here in my bed.
Lady I just cannot get you out of my head.
Lost nights I spent tossing and turning around.
Please come help me get my feet on the ground.
I guess nothing you said was true just all lies.
My heart is breaking, can't you hear its cries?
Lost nights I spent while just being made a fool.
I hope you enjoyed it; did it make you feel cool?
I guess I will lock my heart up with lock and key.
Place it in a bottle toss it out to a stormy Sea.
Lost nights I spent thinking through the night.
Hoping a woman would come treat me right.

CRAZY

A girl I call Crazy I am so glad to know.
It took months for our feelings to show.
She had my heart at the first day.
Now we are together like this today.
Life challenges what is in our heart.
It may just try hard to tear us apart.
We both been hurt enough to know.
To take our time to heal and to grow.
How long will this beautiful feeling last?
Can we just move on and forget the past?
I guess for now we will take our time.
This is for you Crazy your special rhyme.

ABOUT YOU

In the morning I wake up and I think about you.
I feel happy and joyful inside now because of you.
Felt alone and all by myself until I got close to you.
It is a different feeling I have now because I have you.
I found the missing part of me somehow someway.
I love you more because you make me feel this way.
You know every day I just cannot wait to hear from you.
In the morning I wake up "smile" and I think about you.

SHE'S HOT

There is some girl here she's so Hot.
She looks so good with what she got.
She must be the club's hottest looking girl.
Looking so good makes a guy's head whirl.
She hangs at the bar with a girl named Marm.
Sometimes I try too hard to turn on the charm
Maybe this is wrong I wrote this but she's Hot.
I just want to make her smile believe it or not.

NEVER AGAIN

I am never ever falling in love again,
It just hurts me over and over again.
It brings the sun and stops all the pain,
Then love turns dark and brings the rain.
Love always lifts me way up into the sky,
Tosses me out the plane never know why.
Love makes me feel good and then alright,
Then love hurts me keeps me up all night.
Love comes along and mends my heart,
Not long after it just tears me all apart.
Love just hurts me over and over again.
So, I am never ever falling in love again.

TORN APART

I need to share the feelings that is in my heart.
My hearts been bleeding since we been apart.
I feel I have fallen down a long slippery slope
Just hoping soon, you will throw me a rope.
I just want a fresh chance to be a better guy.
Not the guy that broke us and made us cry.
Let us be friends again and just mend our hearts.
My heart cannot stand much more that we are apart.
I thought if I left it would be all better for me.
But I could not get you out from inside of me.
I cannot take this I cannot take this anymore.
Please just give back the key to your door.

SOMETIMES

Sometimes the pain of our past runs deep.
We feel the old hurt as it starts to creep.
We need to be loved and both need it too.
That is why I am writing this poem for you.
Sometimes it is hard to express how we feel.
Is this just a passing or something real?
We are not two ships passing in the night.
This feels way to good it must be right.
Sometimes we are inside each other's minds.
Saying and thinking things at the same time.
We both feel nervous a little scared too.
It is okay sweetheart because I am just like you.
We feel the old hurt as it starts to creep.
Oh, how the pain of our past runs deep.

MY ANGEL

The Mountains is not high, and the Sea is not so wide.
I feel that you are right here next to me at my side.
The Mountain was scary, and the Seas looked too rough,
With you by my side holding my hand it is not so tough.
I can climb that Mountain and cross that rough Sea.
I feel there is an Angel, sent from God to watch over me.
We can climb that Mountain and cross that rough Sea.
I feel deep in my heart that Angel is you I believe it is thee.

UPS AND DOWNS

I know we have had our ups and downs,
Sometimes you just do not want me around.
One thing you can count on that is so true,
No matter what I will always care about you.
You can kick me, yell, scream and just cry,
I will not hate you ever and do not know why.
It is stronger than both of us this glue,
Bonding you to me and me to you.
Sometimes it rattles and almost breaks,
We plow through with some give and take.
There are days we both break down and cry,
This friendship just refuses to up and die.
We do not know how this story will end,
Just remember that I am a good friend.
So, when you feel down or a little blue,
This crazy friend here still likes you.
So, say what you want to do as you please,
Just do not go off and forget about me.
The one who will let you be yourself,
The guy who will never put you on a shelf.
Running out of words to say to you,
I will keep it simple and say I love you.

I FEEL

I feel your tenderness your love and your kindness.
The connection here has a sense of one mindedness.
I will never do a thing to complicate your life.
You already have enough troubles, pain and strife.
So, I just wrote this little silly poem for you.
I feel it was something that I just had to do.
Well, I hope you just had a wonderful great day.
Well, I am back to writing and on my merry way.

I WONDER

When I think of you can't help but wonder.
Will our love blossom or is it a blunder.
When I think of you I see my life unfold.
I'm with you it feels good & I feel bold.
Sometimes I think of you I become afraid.
I fear you'll reject me or I'm being played.
When I think of you I think of love.
You are an angel sent from above.
I think of you & I fear I'll come undone.
Not sure I felt this way about anyone.
When I think of you I think of my past.
Hoping these good feelings will last.
When I think of you, I feel like I could fly
If I ever lost your love, I know I will cry
I woke up this morning tossing in bed.
Thoughts of you were dancing in my head.
Will our love blossom or is it a blunder?
When I think of you cannot help but wonder.

ANGEL IN ME

There is an Angel that I am missing tonight,
How I wish I could squeeze and hold her tight.
I wish I could fill those fingers with mine,
Take some of her heart and make it mine.
Her head is on my shoulder as we lay in bed,
My shoulder just feeling the love in her head.
She may be far but the Angel's in my heart,
The one that has been broken and torn apart.
Maybe these two good hearts can make one,
Place them together laugh and have some fun
Neither of us know what tomorrow will bring,
This sweet Angel just makes me want to sing.
Let me fill those empty spaces in your hand,
As we walk on the beach and kick some sand.
There is an Angel that I am missing tonight,
How I wish I could make her feel exactly right.

THESE FEELINGS

The feeling I got when I saw you here today.
It is hard to describe you just got some way.
You make me feel special & real good inside.
You wake up the feelings I thought had died.
This feeling I get, I do not want it to go away.
I am thinking of you and loving you more today.
Maybe you are thinking I have just lost my mind.
I am writing this to say I love you My Valentine.
My feelings I always share them all with you.
Something in my heart tells me I just have to.
I feel your warm gentle heart inside me now.
I Don't know how but I just feel it somehow.
Good vibes abound when your near me today.
It is hard to describe your just special that way.
Our first Valentine's Day with you was great.
Cannot wait to see you again, I just can't wait,

LET US DO THIS

Let us do this thing even if others think it is wrong.
We can make our own sweet music, sing our own song.
Do we know if the world was to end tomorrow?
Will we part ways happy, alone or in sorrow.
I do not know about you; I want to leave happy.
Sure, do not want to leave feeling alone and crappy.
So, will you please take my hand and walk next to me.
Let us walk in the fire together and let it be.
The fire will keep us warm and it might even burn.
If we do not give this a chance we never will learn.
Let us do this make some music and sing our love song.
What if the fire burns? It will only make us strong.

LOVE IS THIS

Love hurts all the people I like.
But it should never hurt or strike.
Love should stop and listen to me.
Sometimes I wish it would let me be.
Love ignores your deep inner feelings.
Sends your heart broken and reeling.
Love should be back in there now.
Just hurts us over again somehow.
Love should be so kind and special.
Not a trip to the heart hospital.
No tears of love should ever flow.
Love should never let you go.
Love should be a happy good part.
Not a sad broken lonely old heart.
Tell me what is this thing love?
I will have to ask the man above.

MY GIRL

My girl is the sweetest one here.
No one is close or even near.
Her acts of kindness are for real.
Why is she here what is the deal?
Was a broken marriage I see.
She cannot get loose or break free.
I had that same feeling for years.
The broken heart the lonely tears.
Her little, short messages are nice.
Beats off that cold and breaks that ice.
The freezing cold surrounds our hearts.
Just do not let It tear us apart.
It is okay baby just take your time.
I'm running out of words that rhyme.

WHEN A MAN LOVES YOU

When a man loves you, he wants to dance.
He will ask you to dance at every chance.
When a man loves you, he says " Miss You"
Before you leave, he just wants to kiss you.
When a man loves you, it is the little things.
It is not the Gold Jewelry or Diamond rings.
When a man love's you he is truly with you.
Not wandering off with other things to do.
When a man loves you, he wants to dance.
He will ask you to dance at every chance.

THAT MAN

I know that other man broke your heart,
He took your heart and tore it apart.
It did not happen with one big blow,
It was one piece at a time and slow.
Committed, bound and held so tight,
You stayed there and did not feel right.
Scared you would lose valuable things,
The House the Car and Diamond rings.
You hoped he would change for good,
So, you hung on longer than you should.
Then one day you just had about enough,
You stood proud, strong and you got tough.
You left that man who hurt you for years,
Took your things and a bucket of tears.
The pain was in you in so many ways,
You cried many hours it felt like days.
Then one morning the sun was bright,
Everything was good everything was right.
Your fight to break free was not the end,
You broke free so a new life could begin.

PLEASE COME IN

Hey there sweet lady I met do please come in.
Tell me how we happened to meet or begin.
I need some words to write so please come in.
As I peck the keyboard the love story begins.
Maybe someday we will meet so please come in.
Then a special new chapter in our life begins.

WE ARE ONE

We are together and I need to let you know.
How I would feel inside if you ever let me go.
My heart would break do not know what I'd do
The pain would be the thought of losing you.
We have had some good times & shared some bad.
We will always be here when one of us is sad.
You are more than a friend to me, my love
The time we touched I thanked the lord above.
We are together now and hope some years to come
You now have my heart you are my special someone
The way you have held me in your arms this year.
I will always be there for you wipe away the tears.
You have my heart, and I hope I have yours too.
I will stay by your side forever if you want me to.
This poem is a way of showing we are meant to be
When you're ready give me your hand and marry me.

TODAY LOVE

Today I missed that very first text.
Then me missing your voice was next.
I felt all alone deep inside today.
Sweetie I thought about you all day.
I want to share everything in my heart.
My hearts bleeds, it has been torn apart.
I feel I have fallen down a slippery slope
Sweetie I need you to throw me a rope
Please do not think I am like the other guys.
The ones that hurt you and made you cry.
I want to hold you and protect your heart.
Because your heart bleeds when torn apart.
It feels so good when I hear your voice,
I do not have to be sad I now have a choice.
Today I missed that very first text.
Then me missing your voice was next.

THIS WORLD

This bad world might try to tear us apart.
But it cannot get you out of my heart.
It may try to break our sweet bond with lies.
I just wanted you when I opened my eyes.
The world might beat us up with stones.
No matter what you will never be alone.
Sometimes true love takes forever it seems.
The true love that is in your wildest dreams.
The world is a much better place for now.
Now we have found each other somehow.
If this is a dream do not wake me up dear.
It just feels so special to have you here.
The world might just try to tear us apart.
But it cannot get you out of my heart.

SWEETIE

Sweetie you are the best that has happened in my life,
Before that my heart was full of pain and strife.
Our friends and family will probably think we are crazy,
Sweetie we are special, it is the world that is crazy.
The world is filled with so much hate, strife and anger,
Some people are so mean when they meet a stranger.
Somehow through this world full of awfully bad people,
The smoke cleared for two very loving kind people.
Most my life the smoke was just burning my eyes,
Sweetie you rescued me! Did God hear my cries?
Now I want shout to the world "I FOUND YOU!!"
Sweetie I love you, cherish you and care for you.
I want to climb a mountain and yell "SHE IS HERE!!"
Sweetie you cleared the smoke and now I can see clear
I am quickly forgetting all the hurtful pain in my past,
Sweetie you found me a love that will last and last.

DEAR LADY

I know you hurt badly and know how much you cried.
I just want to be here until your tears have all dried.
I want to be the one that helps you heal your heart.
Help you gather up the pieces that were torn apart.
Maybe helping you will fix what is broken within me.
The love and passion bound up needs to be set free.
The easy way out would be to say our last goodbye.
We would never know if it would work if we do not try.
A wise man told me the good things never come easy.
That must be why our hearts are feeling a bit queasy.
I do not know what to say or where we should begin.
Right now, I think, I just cannot wait to see you again.
Lady you just woke up something in my heart today.
Something I was hiding something I had put away.
My poem might be getting a bit mushy and long.
If you really care about someone it cannot be wrong.

WHAT I THOUGHT

I thought she was the lucky one having me around
I lifted her up kept her off the ground
I gave her a reason A purpose to come out
I was there every season like clockwork without doubt
She was the fortunate one getting all my time
All the things I done making sure she was fine
All these things I thought, but in time I truly found
All these things I thought, was the other way around

THANK YOU

Thank you for being my friend I really love you.
But I honestly, I really think there is an Angel in you.
When I see your smile, I feel so wonderful inside.
Maybe you are the one to take me on a magic ride.
I absolutely love making goofy fun with you.
You make me giggle and laugh when you want me to.
I just wrote this silly love poem just for you.
After your gone what else am I supposed to do.

MY HEART

I have given it, and had it given back to me.
It was taken quickly and thrown back at me.
I have held it when I should have given it,
I gave it all away when I should not give it.
It has been loved and broken down in one day.
It was dropped and picked up in the same day.
Please I do not need another sad love story.
Do not be just another broken heart story.
My brain says stop, do not ever let you in.
But my sad heart says to let you right in.
She left my heart for dead on the ground.
Are you the one that turns this all around?
What is done is done what was said was said.
My brain does not want my heart left for dead.
Do not take it if you are going to drop it someday.
Another bump It may not live to see another day.
Will I trust you with my most precious felt part?
Can I? Can I trust? Can I trust you with my heart?

www.ingramcontent.com/pod-product-compliance
Lightning Source LLC
LaVergne TN
LVHW090040080526
838202LV00046B/3903